D1082826

DATE DUE

SUMMER
A Growing Time

by Janet McDonnell
illustrated by Linda Hohag

created by Wing Park Publishers

CHILDRENS PRESS®
CHICAGO

Library of Congress Cataloging-in-Publication Data

McDonnell, Janet, 1962-
Summer, a growing time / by Janet McDonnell ; illustrated by Linda Hohag.
p. cm. — (The Four Seasons)
"Created by Wing Park Publishers."
Summary: Mouse experiences his first summer and hears from the other animals why it is such a wonderful season, filled with plentiful food and the opportunity to grow.
ISBN 0-516-00678-9
[1. Summer—Fiction. 2. Mice—Fiction. 3. Animals—Fiction.] I. Hohag, Linda, ill. II. Title. III. Series.
PZ7.M478436Su 1993
[E]—dc20 93-1182
CIP
AC

Printed in the United States of America.
1 2 3 4 5 6 7 8 9 10 11 12 R 99 98 97 96 95 94 93

SUMMER
A Growing Time

It was a lazy, summer afternoon. The sun was shining, and not a single cloud got in its way. In the shade of a leafy fern, Mouse was just waking up from a long nap. He stretched and yawned.

"I think it's time for a snack," he said. "And I know just where to get it." Mouse scampered out into the field, zig-zagging through clover and grass.

Soon he came to some raspberry bushes. He climbed up a branch and began to nibble on a fat, ripe berry. It was warm and sweet and delicious. As he ate, Mouse looked all around. Pretty butterflies fluttered over the field, and the lovely smell of flowers was in the air.

The sunny day and the sweet snack filled Mouse with energy. Suddenly he saw a grasshopper hop by. "I can catch you, you slowpoke!" said Mouse, and off he ran.

Mouse ran farther and farther out into the field where the grass grew very tall. Soon he had lost the grasshopper.

But with a KERTHUMP! he found Ground Hog. Mouse ran right into him, and both tumbled to the ground. "Oh, sorry, Ground Hog," said Mouse. "I was having so much fun running, I forgot to watch where I was going."

"That's all right," said Ground Hog as they both stood up. "It is a great day for running. I love summer, don't you? It's my favorite season."

"What's summer?" asked Mouse.

"It's this time of year, of course," said Ground Hog.

"Oh. I guess this is my first summer. Should I make it my favorite season, too?"

"You'll have to decide that," said Ground Hog. "But there are many great things about summer. Come on, I'll show you!"

Mouse followed Ground Hog to the top of a tree stump. From there they could see across the whole field.

"Just look at all those flowers, in every color of the rainbow," said Ground Hog. "Summer is the most colorful season of all. That's one reason it is my favorite season."

"That's a good reason," said Mouse.

"I'll show you an even better one," said Ground Hog. "Come on."

"See? In the summertime there are plenty of seeds, berries, clover, and all kinds of yummy food," said Ground Hog. "And they're easy to find."

Mouse was already filling his face with seeds. "Mmm (crunch, crunch, crunch), you're right," he said. "Summer is delicious."

Suddenly, "Look out!" cried Ground Hog. He grabbed Mouse by the tail and pulled him into a nearby burrow. He was just in time, for a big yellow cat pounced out of the tall grass and landed right where Mouse had been sitting.

“Whew! That was a close one!” said Ground Hog. “Summer is great, but it’s not perfect. There is always the danger of hunters who would like to find a summer snack, so be careful.”

Mouse was shaking. “I w-w-will,” he said.

Ground Hog peeked out of the hole. "All clear," he said. "Let's go."

"Maybe we should stay here," said Mouse, "where it's nice and cool — and safe."

"Don't be silly," said Ground Hog. "I have lots more exciting things to show you. We'll be very careful; now come on."

Mouse followed Ground Hog out of the burrow, sniffing and listening for danger.

"Just look at how things grow in the summer," said Ground Hog. "And it's not just plants that grow, you know."

"What do you mean?" asked Mouse.

Just then, they heard, "Look out below!" A young robin came, flapping her wings.

"You're getting better, dear!" Mother Robin called from their nest up above.

"Flying lessons today?" asked Ground Hog.

"Yes," said the young robin. "And I'm going to keep trying until I get them right!"

"See?" Ground Hog said to Mouse. "Baby animals are growing too, and they're learning to do the things that their parents do. Look down there!" He pointed to a bear family

down by the river. "The mama is teaching her babies how to catch fish."

"Wow, those bear cubs sure have gotten big and fat," said Mouse.

As they walked to the river's edge, Mouse and Ground Hog met the Duck family. They were swimming in the warm summer water.

"Well, hello," said Ground Hog. "My, how your children have grown!"

"But what happened to their fuzzy yellow feathers?" asked Mouse.

"Quack, quack," Mother Duck laughed. "My babies are changing," she said. "Soon the girls will look like me, and the boys will look like their father."

As Mouse watched the ducklings climb out of the water and waddle down the path after their mother, his smile slowly turned to a frown.

"What's wrong?" asked Ground Hog.

"Everybody else is growing and changing," said Mouse, "but I'm still the same."

"That's not true," said Ground Hog. "You may not notice it, but you are getting better and better at being a mouse."

"Do you really think so?" asked Mouse.

"I do," said Ground Hog.

By now the sky was growing dark. Lightning bugs began to flash.

"That's another one of my favorite things about summer," said Ground Hog.

Mouse was about to agree when suddenly his whiskers began to twitch. "Watch out!" he cried. He grabbed Ground Hog and pulled him into a hollow log.

Just then, a red fox jumped out of the grass after them! He stuck his snout into the hollow log, but he was too big. He could not reach Mouse and Ground Hog. Soon he gave up and ran off.

"You see?" said Ground Hog. "You are growing up! You're learning how to escape from danger. Thank you for saving me."

Mouse thought about what he had done. He felt proud, and a little bigger than before. Mouse peeked out of the log. "It's safe now," he said in a brave voice.

Just as Ground Hog was crawling out of the log, POW! The sky lit up in an explosion of colors.

"Wow!" said Mouse. "There must be a million lightning bugs up there! How do they make those different colors?"

Ground Hog laughed. "Those are not lightning bugs," he said. "Follow me. I'll show you."

Ground Hog took Mouse to a clearing where lots of people were sitting on the grass, looking up at the sky. When there was a new explosion of colors, they all said, "Oooh," and "Aaah."

"I think people make those colors in the sky somehow," said Ground Hog. "They come out here every year about this time and have a big party."

"I think I know why," said Mouse. "They are celebrating something. And you know what? I want to celebrate too. After all, it's my favorite season. Happy Summer, Ground Hog."

"Happy Summer to you too, Mouse."

You have read what Mouse does in the summer.
Here are some things children do.

Can you read the words?

Can you think of other things?